The Case of the Smiling Shark

TESSA KRAILING

Illustrated by Jan Lewis

D1392090

Oxford University Press

OXFORD
UNIVERSITY PRESS

Great Clarendon Street, Oxford OX2 6DP

Oxford University Press is a department of the University of Oxford.
It furthers the University's objective of excellence in research, scholarship,
and education by publishing worldwide in

Oxford New York

Athens Auckland Bangkok Bogotá Buenos Aires Cape Town
Chennai Dar es Salaam Delhi Florence Hong Kong Istanbul Karachi
Kolkata Kuala Lumpur Madrid Melbourne Mexico City Mumbai Nairobi
Paris São Paulo Shanghai Singapore Taipei Tokyo Toronto Warsaw

with associated companies in Berlin Ibadan

ISBN 0 19 916917 9   School edition
ISBN 0 19 918520 4   Bookshop edition

Printed in Great Britain by Ebenezer Baylis

Illustrations by Jan Lewis

Photo of Tessa Krailing by courtesy of Chris Thwaites

1

Micklesham Pond

This story is about a gang called Foxy and Co. Foxy's real name is Daniel Fox. He looks a bit like a fox, with red hair and a sharp nose. Just the right shape, his dad says, for poking into other people's business.

His best friend is Jamal, sometimes known as Jam-pot.

Jamal is a maths wizard and carries a pocket calculator everywhere. He's always working things out on it. He even worked out how many times their teacher, Mrs Gale, says, 'Honestly, 4G, you're the giddy limit!' Jamal reckons it must be at least six times a day. That is thirty times a week, which is one thousand, two hundred times a year, not counting weekends and holidays.

The third member of the gang is Wesley Clark. He doesn't have a nickname. Everyone reckons that being called Wesley is bad luck enough. Wesley was born unlucky. If a meteorite fell out of the sky on to just one person in the whole wide world, you can bet it would fall on Wesley.

This is the fourth member of Foxy's gang. She's called Marietta. The rest of the gang sometimes try to leave her behind. But mostly they let her come because she makes such a fuss if they don't. And also because she's very brave. This is useful when the gang finds itself in a dangerous situation.

Like the time Mrs Gale asked for volunteers to help clear the litter out of Micklesham Pond.

And Foxy and Co. got bored with clearing litter and decided to look for sharks instead.

And poor Wesley was even unluckier than usual...

'Micklesham Pond is a disgrace,' Mrs Gale told 4G one Friday afternoon. 'Now who'd like to come along next Sunday morning and help me clear it out?'

Not one single person put up their hand.

'Honestly, 4G, you're the giddy limit!' Mrs Gale exclaimed. 'This is your chance to do something for the community. Surely there's someone who'd like to help?'

Foxy shifted uncomfortably in his seat. Mrs Gale was a very forceful person, like her name.

Mostly she blew around Force 5, which was a fresh to moderate breeze, but at this particular moment she was blowing Force 8 and rising.

He had to stop her before she turned into a hurricane.

He put up his hand. 'We'll do it,' he said. 'Me and Jamal and Wesley, we'll help you clear the pond.'

'Splendid!' Mrs Gale beamed at all three of them. 'Meet me on the Common at ten o'clock sharp – and wear your oldest clothes.'

On Sunday morning Foxy was the first to arrive. Micklesham Common was a large, scrubby piece of land surrounded by houses.

At one end lay the pond, shaped like a banana and curving around a clump of trees. Foxy dipped the toe of his wellington boot in the thick white scum lying around the edge. Mrs Gale was right, it was in a terrible state. It was going to take a lot of work.

Jamal arrived next. 'I don't know why you told Mrs Gale we'd help, Foxy,' he grumbled.

Wesley arrived next. The other two stared at him.

'Didn't you hear Mrs Gale tell us to wear our oldest clothes?' Foxy asked.

'Yes, but it's Sunday,' said Wesley.

My Gran always makes me wear my best suit on Sundays.

Wesley had no mother or father, so he had to live with his grandparents. They were older than most people's grandparents and very strict.

At that moment Mrs Gale came jogging up in a red tracksuit.

'Good, you're on time. Any questions before we begin?'

'Just one,' said Foxy. 'Suppose we find something brilliant that's been chucked away, like an old football? Can we keep it?'

'I don't see why not,' said Mrs Gale. 'Right, let's make a start. You tackle this end. I'll get going on the other.' She jogged off around the clump of trees until she was out of sight.

For a while they worked in silence, pulling out all sorts of litter from soggy cardboard boxes to empty beer cans. They passed them back to Wesley, who was keeping well back from the pond.

Suddenly Marietta came flying up. 'There you are! I've been looking for you everywhere. What are you doing?'

'Clearing out the pond,' said Foxy.

'I'll help you,' said Marietta.

She knelt on the bank and leaned over where the water was deepest. It was brown and murky and full of strange ploppings and gurglings. 'I bet there's sharks in there,' she said.

'The chances of finding a shark in that pond,' Jamal said, doing a quick calculation in his head, 'are about one in sixty-five million.'

Just at that moment a shadow, huge
and menacing, darkened the surface of
the pond.

'There's one!' exclaimed Marietta.

The others stared into the water.
Sure enough, staring right back at
them was a shark's face with rows of
pointed teeth and mean little eyes.

AND IT WAS SMILING!

Sunken treasure

'You kids looking for something?' asked the shark.

But the voice didn't come from the pond. It came from behind them.

Foxy and Co. turned to see the shark standing on the bank, smiling toothily. It wasn't really a shark, of course, but a man with shark-like teeth and black oily hair. It must have been his reflection they'd seen in the water.

'We're clearing the pond,' Foxy told him.

'Is that so?' He smiled even wider. 'Then I reckon I'll hang around for a while, to see if you find anything interesting.'

He propped his back against a tree.

Marietta looked at him scornfully. 'You could help us if you wanted,' she said.

That wasn't easy. All the time they worked, Foxy could feel the shark man's mean little eyes watching them. 'What do you think he's after, Jam-pot?' he whispered.

'Don't know,' Jamal whispered back.

Wesley had been getting nearer and nearer the edge of the pond. Just then, he reached out to grab a piece of floating cardboard and lost his balance.

'Oooer,' he shouted, waving his arms around like a windmill. 'I think... I'm going... to... to...'

21

Luckily, the pond was not very deep so Wesley was in no danger of drowning. But when he stood up his face and hands were covered in black sludge. Slimy green weed was clinging to his Sunday suit – and he had a huge grin on his face.

He staggered from the pond, holding out his hand. Foxy and Jamal saw what looked like a lump of mud lying in Wesley's palm. 'What is it?' they asked together.

'Yes, what is it, Wesley?' said Marietta. 'What did you find?'

'Can't you see?' Wesley rubbed off some of the mud to reveal a small round object with a faint metallic gleam.

'It's a coin!' said Foxy.

'It's a *pound* coin,' said Jamal.

'It's sunken treasure,' said Marietta. 'Wesley, you're rich!'

Just then a voice spoke behind
them. It made them jump.

Found something, did you?
Something in the pond?

They had forgotten about the shark
man. Hastily Wesley closed his hand
over the coin and put it behind his
back.

'Just an old button,' said Foxy.
'Somebody must have chucked it away.'

Let's have a look then.

Nobody moved. Marietta said defiantly, 'You can't. It's private. Go away.'

'Hey, that's no way to talk.' The shark man's voice was soft and menacing. He loomed over Wesley. 'Come on, son. No messing about. Show me what you've got in your hand.'

3

Mrs Locket

Suddenly a high, quavery voice called out, 'Is he all right? Is he safe?'

An old lady came hurrying across the Common towards them. Wesley groaned. 'Oh no, it's Mrs Locket. She's a friend of my Gran's.'

She arrived, breathless. 'I saw it happen. I was looking out of my window just as that poor boy fell into the water.'

She peered into Wesley's face. 'My word, it's Wesley Clark – and in your best suit too!'

Wesley was still clutching his precious coin. He looked down at his jacket, which was covered in slimy green weed. 'Er, I don't know...'

'She'll have a fit when she sees you.'
Mrs Locket tutted and shook her head.

You'd better come home with me.
I'll try to clean you up a bit.

And she dragged poor Wesley across
the Common to her house.

The others looked round for the
shark man.

'He's disappeared!' said Foxy.

'He must have run off when he saw Mrs Locket,' said Jamal.

'What a coward,' said Marietta. 'Fancy being scared of a little old lady!'

'We'd better get on with clearing the pond,' said Foxy.

Jamal looked thoughtful. 'Supposing – just supposing – that Marietta was right about the sunken treasure. I mean, Wesley only found one coin.'

Foxy's eyes gleamed. 'You think there might be more?'

'It's possible. And Mrs Gale did say we could keep anything we found.'

'That means we'll ALL be rich,' said Marietta. And she waded into the pond, right up to the top of her boots.

4

The blue china teapot

Meanwhile Wesley was being cleaned up by Mrs Locket. She watched while he scrubbed his face and hands.

Then she took his jacket into the garden to remove the weed.

While she was gone Wesley washed the mud off the pound coin and slipped it into his trouser pocket.

When Mrs Locket came back she handed him his jacket. 'Here you are, Wesley. I've done the best I can. But how on earth did you come to fall into the water?'

Wesley shrugged. 'It's because I'm unlucky, I suppose.' He touched the coin in his pocket. 'At least, usually I am.'

Mrs Locket sighed. 'I've been unlucky too. Yesterday a young man came to the door and offered to dig my garden. I said yes because my back's been bad lately and digging's hard work.

'When he'd finished I asked him in for a cup of tea. Next thing I knew, he'd run off with my teapot.'

'Oh, not the old brown teapot I use for making the tea. No, this was my special blue china teapot. The one I keep my savings in.

'Of course I chased after him. Chased him halfway across the Common, as far as the pond. But then I lost him.' Mrs Locket's lip started to tremble.

'Did you tell the police?' Wesley asked.

'Of course. I told them exactly what he looked like. Mean little eyes he had and pointed teeth.'

Wesley stared at her.

'Exactly like a shark. But I don't suppose they'll ever find him. When I think of him getting away with my blue teapot I could – I could – ' Mrs Locket looked quite fierce. 'I could *thump* him!'

'Perhaps he didn't get away with it.
Perhaps he dropped it when you
chased after him.' Again Wesley
touched the coin in his pocket.

'Mrs Locket, this money you had in
the blue china teapot – was it notes...
or in coins?'

Coins,
over thirty
pound coins.

'I'd been saving them out of my
pension to pay the electricity bill,'
continued Mrs Locket. She wiped her
eyes with her handkerchief. 'Now I
shall never see them again.'

Wesley sighed.

Somehow he'd known it was too good to be true. He took his hand out of his pocket and gave the coin to Mrs Locket.

'Here's one of them,' he said. 'And I think I know where we can find the rest.'

5

'Gordon, stand still!'

'I've found something!' Marietta fished
a browny-blue object out of the water.
'It's hard – and round – and it's got a
sort of spout at one end.'

'It's just a dirty old teapot,' said
Jamal. He lay on his stomach, peering
into the pond.

Marietta scrambled up the bank and showed the teapot to Foxy. 'It feels heavy... and listen.'

She shook it. It made a rattling noise. 'It sounds as if there's a lot of little stones inside.'

Foxy peered into the pot.

I don't think they're stones. I think they're . . .

But before he could finish, a large hand swooped down and tried to snatch the teapot from Marietta's grasp. 'That's mine,' growled the shark man, appearing from the bushes.

Marietta clutched it tightly. 'It's not yours, it's mine. Go away, you big bully.'

'She's right,' said Foxy. 'Mrs Gale said we could keep anything we found. So it's our teapot. We found it.'

'And now you've lost it!' The shark man grabbed the teapot out of Marietta's hands and ran off with it.

At the same moment Wesley and Mrs Locket came hurrying across the Common. 'There he is!' cried Mrs Locket. 'That's the man. Stop, thief!'

The shark man heard her voice and glanced over his shoulder.

He didn't see Jamal's legs lying across the path. Next moment he went sprawling headlong.

The teapot flew through the air. It landed on the hard ground and smashed to pieces, scattering its contents.

Jamal sat up to take a closer look. 'Hey, those aren't stones!' he said. 'They're – '

'Pound coins!' Wesley arrived, panting. 'He stole them from Mrs Locket. Quick, stop him!'

The shark man jumped to his feet and took off like a rocket round the clump of trees.

And he came face to face with Mrs Gale.

'Gordon Fowler!' she exclaimed. 'What on earth are you doing here?'

She looked past him. There was Mrs Locket shaking her fist and Jamal rubbing his leg that had just been tripped over.

'Still causing trouble, by the look of it,' she continued sternly. 'You haven't changed since you were in my class ten years ago.'

The shark man, alias Gordon Fowler, started to back away. But at that moment Mrs Gale bellowed, 'Gordon, STAND STILL!'

And amazingly he did.

Now, will somebody please tell me what's going on?

Everyone spoke at once.

Somehow Mrs Gale managed to make sense of it all. 'Honestly, Gordon, you're the giddy limit,' she said.

6

The shark's mum

The shark man looked scared. 'No, please – don't call the police. My mum will be furious if she finds out.'

'Ah yes, I remember your mum,' Mrs Gale said, nodding her head. 'And I can imagine just how furious she's going to be. But I'm afraid you should have thought of that before you stole Mrs Locket's teapot.'

'The police are already looking for him,' said Wesley. 'Mrs Locket told them what he looks like.'

'Yes, I did,' said Mrs Locket. 'I told them he had black oily hair and mean little eyes.'

'In that case,' said Mrs Gale, 'I reckon it won't be long before you're caught, Gordon.'

The shark man looked more than scared. He looked terrified.

'Please, Mrs Gale,' he begged. '*Please* don't call the police. I'll do anything you ask.'

'That's up to Mrs Locket.' Mrs Gale turned to the old lady. 'What do you think?'

Mrs Locket looked uncertain. 'Well, I suppose… if he promises never to do such a thing again…'

Mrs Gale turned back to the shark man. 'Do you promise?'

He gulped. 'I promise.'

'Very well, Gordon. The first thing I want you to do is pick up all those pound coins lying around. Give them back to Mrs Locket.

'Oh, and don't forget to tell her you're sorry.'

The shark man got down on his hands and knees. He started scrabbling about in the mud. When he had collected all the coins he handed them over to the old lady, muttering, 'Sorry, Mrs Locket.'

Mrs Locket accepted the coins – and the apology – with a gracious nod of her head.

'Right,' said Mrs Gale briskly. 'Now I want you to go down to the Sunday market. You can buy her a brand new teapot to make up for the one you broke. Understand?'

Yes, Mrs Gale.

He sounded quite meek and mild, more like a tadpole than a shark.

'Well, hurry up, then! What are you waiting for?'

'Nothing, Mrs Gale. I'm going, Mrs Gale.'

He hurried off across the Common as if a police dog was already panting at his heels.

Mrs Gale waited until he had disappeared before turning to Wesley.

'As for you, Wesley,' she said with a sigh, 'I think you'd better go straight home and have a hot bath.'

Wesley groaned. 'My Gran'll be hopping mad,' he muttered.

Mrs Locket continued, 'Because I shall come with you. I'll tell her how you helped me get my money back. She can't possibly be mad with you then. In fact I want you to have some kind of a reward. How about the biggest ice cream you've ever seen?'

Wesley cheered up at once. 'Could it be vanilla with chocolate sauce?'

'Whatever you like.'

Wesley's eyes lit up. It looked as if his luck had turned at last.

When they had gone Jamal said, 'Fancy the shark man being at our school ten years ago.'

'Yes, and he must have been as mean and nasty then as he is now,' said Marietta. 'But he's really scared of his mum, isn't he?'

'If his mum is the Mrs Fowler who lives down Rosamund Street I'm not surprised,' said Jamal. 'She's as big as a rhino and twice as fierce.'

'Poor Gordon,' Marietta sighed. 'I almost feel sorry for him, living in the same house as a rhino. Even if he *is* a shark.'

Foxy grinned.

About the author

I wrote my first story at the age of four. From that moment I knew I wanted to be a writer, but it was many years before my first book, (which was about dinosaurs) was published. Since then, I have written over thirty  books for children of all ages. Best of all I love writing mystery stories and stories that make people laugh.

I got the idea for this story while helping to clear out a pond on the Isle of Wight, where I now live.

Other Treetops books at this level include:

I Wish, I Wish by Paul Shipton
The Personality Potion by Alan MacDonald
The Goalie's Secret by Paul Shipton
The Ultimate Trainers by Paul Shipton
Waiting for Goldie by Susan Gates

Also available in packs
| *Stage 13 pack B* | 0 19 916918 7 |
| *Stage 13 class pack B* | 0 19 916919 5 |